Crazy Thoughts

Naturally Curious

Saroj Kumar Mallick

 pencil

ISBN 978-93-5458-220-2
© Saroj Kumar Mallick 2021
Published in India 2021 by Pencil

A brand of

One Point Six Technologies Pvt. Ltd.
123, Building J2, Shram Seva Premises,
Wadala Truck Terminal, Wadala (E)
Mumbai 400037, Maharashtra, INDIA
E connect@thepencilapp.com
W www.thepencilapp.com

Author biography

A recent incident in my life changed the ME and they way I look at everything. One should always do what you wish for and it does not really matter unless it gives you happiness and Love... **Be CRAZY, Be YOURSELF,**Unwind yourself to this beautiful place called WORLD and experience the *Beauty called LIFE & LOVE...*

CONTENTS

Soil

It is a **CRAZY** time,
Where roaming outside is a crime,
Everything was so beautiful,
People of earth were not so dull,
Everyone was having so much fun,
Even travelling was filled with fun,
In the late last year we got hit,
Which made the earth stop in its pit,
Many departed and got split,
Everyone is praying to stay fit,
The beautiful planet of ours has become dark,
An invisible ailment is roaming like a shark,
Masks, sanitizers, distancing will take us out of this dark,
A lot of mortals are facing the sudden dangerous doom,
Mother earth is crying to take them into her womb,
Suited in white & khaki ALMIGHTY created warriors,
They are our sole saviors,
Oh Lord! let there be a new dawn,
Let there be a new ray of sun,
Braveheart's are trying hard to have the shark tamed,
Mankind will certainly again be famed,
Almighty! please bless us to fight this battle royal,
To keep the living, non-living stay on this beautiful
SOIL...

You & Me

The memories of that **CRAZY** winter are still vivid,
When I remember them, it reminds me of being together,
On Friday night our eyes met,
On Saturday we got close,
On Tuesday it became certain,
On Friday night it repeated,
We were in a haze and fell in love,
I wanted to believe that that was fate,
Morning, I was a little shy
Lunch time, you're so cute
Sunset, you're beautiful
That winter with all our hearts,
Became we from **YOU & ME...**

Rain

It was the **CRAZY**night we were supposed to meet,
I asked myself a question,
Am I really anticipating something?
If I have left with a little bit of happiness,
If I have left with a little bit of satisfaction,
I will lose myself in the same place,
I don't know if it's a real situation,
I reacted to everything,
Although that's a contradiction,
In a Dream I saw a future,
That we were together,
All my feelings hurt,
With a lot of Pain,
When my love faded,
In that night of **RAIN...**

Long Drive

I'll try and make your **CRAZY** dream come true,
I'll put wings on you so you can fly,
I'll stand by you forever and ever,
If I become a lost child in your heart,
If I become a lost soul in your life,
Please do not get angry,
Take me to the origin of love,
Where I see you my Goddess of Beauty,
And your beautiful stunning smile,
When you & Me are on a **Long Drive...**

Straight Talk

You say you are good and **CRAZY** satisfied,
But your body tells me something else,
You say you are truly thrilled,
But your voice tells me something else,
You say you are never terrified
But your eyes tell me something else,
I am watching your body talk,
I am watching your tears walk,
I am watching your beautiful smile drop,
What is it, my baby?
Come, let's go on a long and lonely walk,
Where we can have **Straight Talk...**

Pain

In this **CRAZY**Life of mine,
I don't need you anymore in my life,
I still wet my pillow every night,
Avoiding single ray of light,
I lived in fear everyday,
Thinking that you will leave me one day,
Hold my breath again,
Hold my hand again,
Hold my forehead again,
Hug me again,
Kiss me again,
Oh My Baby you departed this earth,
Leaving me alone,
To spend my life in this **PAIN...**

Fantasy

I know you now for a **CRAZY** amount of time,
Your body still feels nice and warm to me,
The sun feels beautiful & warm,
The lake is showing its charm,
The winter feels nice & cool,
The mountains are becoming blue,
When you were there with me,
When you were close to me,
When I hugged you,
When I kissed you,
You left your fear,
Whispering in my ear,
I want you to be beside me,
I want you to be within me,
The world should glow with jealousy,
When you are with me and That's my **FANTASY...**

Whisper

There are many **CRAZY** things in life I can endure,
One important thing is not being your,
Which I can not even cure,
I know I am not doing my best,
To be your dearest,
I know I am not full of love & care,
To be your pair,
But I will try again,
Till I hit the mountain,
To take away all your pain,
Till it pours me with your love rain,
I will hold my breath,
Until my death,
Until you become mine,
And together in we shine,
Together in care we prosper,
When I scream in love, you **WHISPER...**

Shadow

I had a dream of a **CRAZY**girl,
Who looked like a fresh pearl,
She waves her hand to try to reach me,
But I could not set myself free,
I wish I knew what she says,
I wish I knew what she wants,
I wish I knew what she expects,
Her beautiful smile shined,
Her marvelous hair grinds the wind,
Her gorgeous appearance was not to slip one's mind,
Her lovely soul had a touch of kind,
I desperately want to be with her,
To make my whole life clear,
To make the whole world blur,
I want to go back to that dazzling dream show,
Where you and me were together like a **SHADOW...**

Walk

Where do you wanna spend the **CRAZY**eternity?
Loving all the way to infinity,
Searching for serenity,
We were into each other,
When we were together,
There was a lot of passion,
Diverting all the diversions,
Let's raise our relation curtain,
Removing the chain,
Overcoming the pain,
Hold my hand again,
Let's be together again,
Let's create our own life,
Where I can call you my wife,
You will be my respect,
Our life will be so perfect,
Let us stop that clock,
When we go on our love **WALK...**

Kiss

When I was young I was **CRAZY**,
As I was always being so lazy,
When I became an adult,
Madness came out of my vault,
Till I saw an angel,
Who changed my life angle,
She walked with me,
She stood by me,
She cared for me,
She made love to me,
She is my world,
Keeping my life twirled
Who kept me thrilled,
To have you in my life is a bliss,
You are the only one I **KISS...**

Pray

It's been **CRAZY**hard,
To take the invisible sword,
To be lost in the unknown wizard,
Now, everything looks dark,
Where, there is no spark,
She is my life who could not speak,
She is my love who could not walk,
She is my darling who could not touch,
Oh Baby... I Love You So Much,
So many words swallowed,
So many thoughts bowed,
Oh Love to be together we vowed,
Sound of wind is unheard,
Ray of sun feel awkward,
Without you everything looks gray,
You come back to life,
That's my only **PRAY**...

Hope

I had a **CRAZY** pounding in my heart,
Because I am not that smart,
To make you my Sweet Heart,
Breaking the dark of night,
Disappearing the fake light,
Like a star full of bright,
Comes Princess of Beauty,
Who is mesmerizing and cutie,
To look at her my eyes tumble,
To talk to her my tongue tremble,
To be with her my legs stumble,
I want to walk her down to aisle,
With her pure and beautiful smile,
In the company of her fabulous style,
Expressed my love to her in an envelope,
She would accept it with love,
is my only **HOPE...**

Hug

I can't beat my **CRAZY**heart,
I just want to be with you my sweet heart,
But, till the war is over we need to stay apart,
We are at damn war,
Soldiers are showing their valor,
To be superior,
Oh Lord! we want peace,
Come and shower your divine grace,
If I get hit by a bullet,
Please do check my wallet,
If it's not drenched with my blood,
If it's not become dirty with mud,
I have kept a letter for you,
Which will take you through,
I have promised to come back,
Alive or covered in wooden plank,
My Love! Please don't be in tear,
Have absolutely no fear,
Take yourself a great care,
I swear I am always there,
It's time for my grave to be dug,
Oh My Love! if you could actually give me a **HUG...**

Sky

I always love you in my **CRAZY** soul,
Your presence makes my life whole,
Your beautiful eyes got my heart stole,
Making me feel like a goldfish in the bowl,
My life had absolute no vision,
Had a lot of dreams with confusion,
Your existence cleared my delusion,
Falling in love with you is my only confession,
Life was amazing and going good,
Had a lot of love and happiness mood,
But the Creator had other plan,
Making me a lone man,
Within a very short span,
I urge an answer to my why,
Requesting the Supreme Almighty,
When I look at **SKY...**

Magic

It was a beautiful & **CRAZY** dawn,
I was in the sweet dream of my own,
Where I could stand in front of the moon,
A gorgeous girl came out of the light,
Shining like a star very bright,
Her beauty can illuminate the entire night,
She looked stunning in baby pink dress,
I was desperate to make her impress,
She had a decorative mark in the middle of her forehead,
Her mesmerizing beauty can have any mountain mislead,
Her hands were filled with bangle,
Nature was dancing in those sweet jingle,
Her heavenly legs had anklets,
Which looked like my life booklet,
She had her hair open,
By now I was awestruck & driven,
There was light in my room,
Flowers were about to bloom,
Suddenly my eyes are wide open,
It was beautiful dream which got broken,
I pray to GOD to do some trick,
If I meet my Dream Girl, that'll be a **MAGIC...**

Mother

When I came to this **CRAZY**World,
You had me furled,
You had answers to all your whys
When you looked in to my eyes,
You taught me sincerity,
With complete loyalty,
So that I can establish my authority,
Keeping intact my integrity,
To touch the sky with prosperity,
You skipped your meals,
Because I should not be on kneels,
You did a mammoth of adjustment,
Laughingly taking all embarrassment,
Thought of you not being in my life,
Cuts my throat with an ultra sharp knife,
I am incapable of clearing your debt,
No matter how much I spare blood & sweat,
You are the strongest I have ever seen,
For me who can stand bare hand in the frontline,
Presence of yours gives me power,
All my questions get their answer,
Please fill me up with your bless shower,
Even Almighty looks up to her,
We call her **MOTHER...**

Anger

I know I had been **CRAZY**My Darling,
Falling miserably to be caring,
Coz of me all our plans are cancelling,
But trust me baby I will make it up to you,
Please don't feel pale blue,
I promise to be a changed man,
Within a very short span,
Please give me a last chance,
To clear out the distance,
To ignite the fire of romance,
To fill you up with love fragrance,
I swear to give you time,
I vow to make you completely mine,
No presence of you is a torturous feel,
Which is impossible for me to heal,
It feels like it stopped my life wheel,
I obviously don't have nerves of steel,
Please wake up and wear you pink suit,
In which you look incredibly cute,
Help me come out of this danger,
Which I call it is your **ANGER...**

Fear

My Love! we have spent some **CRAZY**moment,
With a numerous amount of love and attachment,
To each other, we have given our life commitment,
We saw each other,
We liked each other,
We Love each other,
We had many fights,
Were away from each other's sight,
Together everything seemed right,
We had the prize of our warmth,
Which kept us running back n forth,
I understand we are now staying apart,
With a heavy and patient heart,
Oh My Love! I miss you a lot,
I swear we will tie the knot,
Be patient and brave,
We will pass through this wave,
And will be inseparable till the grave,
There will be sun rise,
Together we will make new memories,
Please get up, smile and cheer,
Almighty will bless us to be together,
It wont happen, please don't be in that **FEAR...**

Life

Unconsciously, I have been walking **CRAZY**,
With memories becoming hazy,
Down in this long and narrow road
Thinking of my reminiscence to explode,
If I look back, far off in the distance,
It felt like a test of tolerance,
Filled with uneven, twisting and turning road,
I was strangled like a messy chess board,
Still it felt like a flow of river,
I had nothing to fear,
Everything was great and so amazing,
With bright and shine lights glowing,
Self Existence put me on to a test,
Inserting a bullet in to my chest,
All lights came shattering down,
Making me a laughing clown,
Struggled and stood up again,
Breaking the odd controversy chain,
Life was becoming okay,
With soothing light of ray,
Almighty had other plan,
Making me realize existence has a short span,
Be always with your loved ones,
Spreading care & love in tons,
Please don't keep any strife,

Enjoy and cherish every single time,
This is what we call is **LIFE...**

Heaven

We have had our **CRAZY** time,
Loving each other felt like crime,
It was hell of a struggle,
To get into a lovely snuggle,
We had many fight,
Fragmenting our warmth light,
Our love stood strong,
Making right every wrong,
We walked on a beautiful path,
Living on each other's breath,
We made it through my sunshine,
Now everything looks fine,
It's time for us to take our vow,
My Darling! We are inseparable now,
Let's take everyone's bless,
For making our love success,
I thank The Almighty,
For making us together with dignity,
We will now be always together,
In the world of another,
Where only we both are each other's companion,
A beautiful place which we call **HEAVEN...**

Honeymoon

Its a **CRAZY** time for both of us,
Clearing out all unbalanced dusts,
We obviously are in a lot of blush,
Both of us have a beautiful adrenaline rush,
We are now with each other,
Vowed to be always together,
Your touch has a sense of cure,
Feels like a morning azure,
We are in each other's arm,
Making this moment lighted with love charm,
When I kiss your beautiful lips,
A lovely passion grips,
We come close,
To each other's expose,
We have ignited the passion of romance,
Thank you for giving me your acceptance,
There is no space between us for the wind to pass by,
Even under the marvelous naked sky,
There's only warmth of each other to be felt,
Let's both of us be together with passion and melt,
I am mesmerized with your plain appearance,
Filled with your spectacular fragrance,
I don't want this passionate time to pass soon,
When you and me are in our **HONEYMOON...**

Dance

It was a beautiful **CRAZY** city,
Making me feel amazing & hearty,
I came here to join my new duty,
Trying to absorb it's mesmerizing beauty,
Next day I go to my work,
It was in the middle of a tech park,
Suddenly, I saw an elegant spark,
Coming out of the dark,
She looked like a pearl white star,
She stood a little far,
Her voice sounded like tune of sitar,
She asked me my introduction,
So that she could provide work instruction,
Looking at her I was in my own world,
My heart popped out and was felling thrilled,
Days, Weeks, Months pass by,
It was time to say good bye,
I have not told anything to her,
Because of my own foolish fear,
She is the one who took away my sleep,
I had nothing do than just weep,
Few months after our family went to see a girl,
She looked exactly like the same pearl,
It was the same fragrance,
Which imbalanced my life balance,

She was the same pearl white star,
That day who stood a little far,
I am overwhelmed with her beauty & elegance,
Now, between us there is only romance,
People always look at us with envious glance,
In love & affection, when we both **DANCE...**

Society

We have a **CRAZY** amazing love bond,
Which is unbelievable and beyond,
We both care for each other,
Irrespective of any weather,
We have spent a lot of good time,
Where we were partners in crime,
A small complication can not separate us,
Certainly can not create a ruckus,
Remember those days when we had amazing fun,
Together we had the ability to stand in front of a gun,
I know there will be a lot more complication,
Love & Trust will be our foundation,
Together in warmth we stand,
Holding each other's hand,
Let any issues come by,
Together will fight till we die,
I get it, will be tough to marry,
Trust me it will be a wonderful story,
Between us let there be only romance,
Between us let there be no distance,
There will be concerns in variety,
Which will create a lot of anxiety,
We will only show respect, love & sobriety,
To this fantastic place called **SOCIETY...**

Sunshine

I am hit by cupid's **CRAZY**arrow,
Which made my compassion grow,
You have stolen my heart,
Our love is about to start,
I want to be in your embrace,
Keep looking at your angel like face,
I want to be melted in your dark eyes,
Like the clouds in the skies,
I want to be held like a child,
My heart trembled when looked at me & smiled,
I want to fall asleep in your arms,
Like a drop of water on the cold morning farms,
You set a fire in my heart darling,
Which keeps my heart burning,
My heart is nervous,
Being very anxious,
Praying to Almighty,
Give me strength to act mighty,
To Walk up to you,
To give you my love clue,
I really can't even if I try,
Can't make you the apple of my eye,
I now belong to the promised land,
Which does not allow me a firm stand,

I wish I could make you mine,
Praying to GOD for that **SUNSHINE...**

Need

On a warm, **CRAZY** sunny day,
By the mesmerizing sea bay,
Under the bright blue sky,
I met a beautiful girl,
She had her hair curl,
It was love at first sight,
Making everything seem so right,
I told her about my love,
I expressed her my feeling,
Oh love!!! will you be my darling,
I will stand by your side,
Swim against any imbalance tide,
I will always love you,
Till my breath bids adieu,
She looked stunningly amazed,
By her my face was getting gazed,
She smiled and walked away,
Doubtful I was looking at her leaving in sway,
Years past by,
Under the same bright sky,
Now I call the same beautiful girl my wife,
She is the breath of my life,
She is my life's happiness seed,
Her presence is what I always **NEED...**

Bond

When I look at you my face gets **CRAZY**red,
Love ignites from heels till head,
When I look at you I just smile out of nowhere,
Your smile inserts my heart like a sphere,
When I see you I feel like I am up on the clouds,
Away from impenetrable crowd,
You're the president of my heart,
Who makes my life an art,
You make me stop breathing,
Your presence is so soothing,
There's no reason for my love you know,
As days pass, it would only grow,
You are more beautiful than stars above in the sky,
You are more blinding than the sunlight up in the sky,
Your sweet voice makes the feather fly,
Our struggle was immense when we were staying apart,
Even though both of us were living in one single heart,
All our dark phases have came to an end,
Together let's thank GOD and have our life spend,
Let's ignite the fire of romance,
Let the world mesmerize our love fragrance,
The moment of our ordinary days became special,
As we became precisely official,

On the course we fought a lot,
Still at the end we tied the knot,
It was our love which kept us going beyond,
An invisible superpower, I call it **BOND...**

Hostel

It definitely is a **CRAZY** place,
Which has its own peace,
Life runs here with overflowing pace,
It prepares us to become an ace,
Everyone leaves their family for it,
At beginning it makes us feel unfit,
Few even call it a quit,
Who stay, it makes their life a super hit,
Our anger has no value here,
No matter we hold a sword or sphere,
In the end we adjust to its atmosphere,
So that in life we can be a torch bearer,
It gives us many memories,
Stealing good food become our glories,
Birthdays become ultimate fear day,
Kicking our bottom people make us cry,
We forget the word called shy,
Over here everyday is a festival,
We learn tips and tricks of survival,
Partying gets a new amazing look,
It has everything apart from book,
Crying gets forbidden,
Fear gets hidden,
This becomes our very own world,
Where we are the underworld,

Everyone gets a new nick name,
Which gets us the ultimate fame,
Slangs become new way of speaking,
Where we learn everything,
Almost from very beginning,
Prepares us to be Queen & King,
King of demon bows in this hell,
I call this amazing place **HOSTEL...**

Faith

We were in our **CRAZY**love,
Felt like we were all of the above,
Together we were strong and brave,
When we got hit by the cold wave,
You made me complete,
Felt like my heart missed a beat,
In my life you turn up the heat,
My love... You are so sweet,
You are my life's honor,
You are my existence's governor,
You are my life's respect,
Thank you for being my soul architect,
I remember I wished one day,
I will take you above the sky,
Never thought my wish will be granted this way,
Letting me live only in hope and pray,
I love the way we fight,
When I hug you real tight,
Now I am living my life in a fright,
As my soul architect has gone out of sight,
You are my life's pride,
Would you please be my bride,
Now this is my only crave,
Weeping in front of your grave,

Praying to GOD to return your warmth,
Keeping nothing but only **FAITH...**

41

Father

What a **CRAZY** time it was,
Summer felt you like Christmas,
You were the happiest in earth,
Hearing the news of my birth,
Happiness tear rolled down your eyes,
Making me your own beloved prize,
You held me in your arm,
My eyes glittered in your happiness charm,
You taught me how to dream,
You taught me how to swim against the stream,
You made me understand what's confidence,
You showed me how to prevail in excellence,
You are awake all day and night,
So that I can fill my life with light,
My safety & happiness is your only dream,
For that you don't even hesitate to turn the beam,
I know you always have my back,
You will not wait to slap if I go off track,
You will always put me in to comfort,
Keeping aside all your discomfort,
Presence of you gives me identity,
Your hand on me puts me to serenity,
Even Almighty needs your presence,
To prove the very existence,

I know I have never told earlier,
Love you forever **FATHER...**

Void

What a **CRAZY** time we had together,
Your touch was like a feather,
You made me feel like a mother,
Wish I could change the autumn weather,
We made a lot of memories,
Moving beyond boundaries,
I love it when I snuggle with you,
Not sure how time flew,
It was nothing but just pure love,
Which will always stand all of the above,
Your presence was something amazing,
Which kept my life buzzing,
Thought of your unavailability is unacceptable,
My feelings for you is indescribable,
I love the way you hold, kiss & look at me,
Which provided me the power to be free,
You moved to other world making me alone,
Putting me forever in debt in your love loan,
A millennium and half long relation,
How will I fill the empty duration,
Thinking of the same makes me paranoid,
My heart will always be in this **VOID...**

Dawn & Dusk

This **CRAZY** time won't come again,
This atmosphere won't be cast again,
We won't meet like this again,
Who knows what will happen later,
Whether we will meet here after,
I know that we'll be on separate paths after a while,
Till then let's make it our own aisle,
Let me walk with you till that time,
I am cold without you, I am coming to you,
All of this feels so untrue,
Everything is on fire,
You are my ultimate desire,
Your eyes are unbroken universe like Narnia,
Your touch feels like cool breeze in the bay of California,
Loose them in the dark,
Let us ignite our spark,
Let us enlighten this moment,
Love & Care is my only commitment,
You are the Queen of My existence,
I am baffled by your elegance,
I go down on my knees and ask,
Will you marry me keeping witness this **DAWN & DUSK...**

King & Queen

It must be a **CRAZY** day,
When both of us had our 1st cry,
Everyone must be in a lot of joy,
Pronouncing us a girl & a boy,
We grew up next to each other,
Being in nursery as back bencher,
We went to the same school,
Playing & fighting were our only tool,
We even went to the same university,
To be friends with the diversity,
We both had our own brake up,
Drinking alcohol in coffee cup,
We got our placements,
It was time to work for the clients,
We were making a lot of adjustments,
Finding each other's replacements,
That's when we realize we miss our fights,
Which broke many lights,
We miss our together drinking,
listening to each other's drunk barking,
We miss our trust,
Which made a lot of them bite the dust,
We miss our happiness,
Which use to fill our emptiness,
Years pass by, it's time for us to be together again,

I am sure we will have a lot to explain,
Let's just look at each other and enjoy the scene,
To be called as each other's **KING & QUEEN...**

Wings

Life now a days tells a **CRAZY** story,
Encourages to take the ultimate glory,
It's telling me that if you listen to me then walk,
It's time for you to be on the block,
Walk in the paths of your dreams,
Creating your own unbreakable themes,
Take all the fragrances & all the light,
Make the world mesmerizingly bright,
The days and the nights are all new,
The emotions are all new,
The desires are all new,
The new paths are for you,
Then why do you stay in this shelter,
Why do you stand behind a filter,
The earth and the sky are new for you,
Let the world have your success view,
Write a phenomenal new story in the air,
With an absolute care and flair,
All the windows of your heart will open up,
All those silences will get dissolved up,
All the identities will open up,
Fill them up in your eyes,
It's time for you to touch the sky,
It's time for you to pull the strings,
It's time for you to open your **WINGS...**

Betrayal

Those were the **CRAZY** great days,
Which caused everyone's eyebrows raise,
Together we were strong as mountain,
Which had only our romance fountain,
The entire colony used to echo with our love,
For me you were all of the above,
We counted the stars in the moonlit night,
Igniting our passion & taking it to a new height,
My life was just like a dream,
Which was filled with your sweet love cream,
Oh my Love! there was only love between us,
Before you caught that bus,
All my memories have come fresh just by seeing you,
All of sudden a bolt hit from the blue,
You told me the fake stories of fake faithfulness,
You told me the fake stories of fake love-ness,
Even GOD was not true for me,
Instead you were true for me,
Nowadays I twist and turn on my bed,
Whenever your thought comes to my head,
I realized the path I was travelling,
Will put me through hot boiling,
Still I pray for your happiness,
Your life should not have any darkness,
Till today you're a part of my memories,

Tears for you are present in my eyes,
Even today in the gatherings,
Thought of you put me through burning,
I still have all the wounds,
Which puts me to a scary ground,
Unbelievable to digest your love portrayal,
When I am a sufferer of your **BETRAYAL...**

Beauty

She is so **CRAZY**magnificent,
World has been enthralled in her scent,
I know that there are marks on the moon,
But she is a mark less divine boon,
She is so amazingly marvelous,
GOD has taken time to make her fabulous,
I know we cant love angles,
It will be a sin to not to wait for those jingles,
I tried to stop it for a million times,
Your angle persona in my head always climbs,
In the aspirations of those moments,
A pure feel of warmth foments,
May I always remain colored in Your colors,
May I always remain splendorous,
You are an Almighty handcrafted cutie,
Who has the potential to move the world off duty,
With her majestic & breathtaking **BEAUTY...**

Sunlight

You are my **CRAZY** unsatisfied thirst,
Without whom my life becomes worst,
The condition of my heart is of total obsession,
Being in love with you to GOD is my only confession,
You have become dearest to me,
Please come close to me,
Just always be with me,
If you say yes then my soul will escape like a waterfall,
Summer will have a beautiful snowfall,
There'll be shower of pearls on the roads of our journey,
Be my life's ultimate attorney,
I am walking with dreams as delicate as glass,
Your presence in it makes it a first-class,
I am in constant fear of collision,
Your faith in me will give a vision,
The flame of hope is still burning,
Loneliness is stinging me and my heartbeats are rising,
To come out of the dark I am still praying,
I plea for only one Affirmation,
You be my strongest foundation,
Your soul is filled with bright light,
You are the one who gives me courage to fight,
Do you mind being my **SUNLIGHT**...

College

It was my **CRAZY** first day,
I was a lot scared & shy,
It was a new beginning of my life,
Not sure who is standing there with a knife,
I will certainly become something,
That's what I have been promising,
Everyone says these are going to be the best days,
It will be filled with marvelous joys,
Years passed by being in the same place,
It made me ready for the life race,
I was fortunate to spend healthy five years here,
Which certainly makes my existence steer,
Still remember the 1st day scare and the last day cry,
It was really hard to say good bye,
Still remember the canteen fights,
Drinking in the coffee mug in broad day light,
Bunking the room was a state of an art,
Getting caught was the worst part,
Many hearts were broken,
Many stayed unbroken,
It taught us true meaning of friendship,
Definitely a lot about relationship,
A place which bestows the ultimate knowledge,
Everyone calls it a **COLLEGE...**

You

Yesterday was a **CRAZY** day,
When I came across sorrows on the way,
I hugged the sorrows and wept,
Even though it was tough for me to accept,
Something which was mine & only mine,
Is now near the holy shrine,
Those pair of eyes whom I used to kiss without any
reason,
Which kept me going in all season,
Why in those eyes there's no love left for me anymore?
Why all of a sudden everything has become sore?
The feeling which saddens my heart all the time,
Earlier she was the reason behind the smile,
The sleep once left me, didn't return anymore,
It has immensely darken the door,
So many nights have been perished,
There is only memories now to be cherished,
Oh dear! she was my last drop of tear,
Which got vanished in to a thin air,
I keep on loving her even in her absence,
Certainly interrogates my love existence,
Why there is a test of my love?
I am definitely not that brave,
Please come to me from somewhere,
Eagerly waiting for love & care,

Feels like a bullet hit from the blue,
Tell me how can I live without **YOU???**

55

Heart

It was a **CRAZY**awesome weather,
When I came across a beautiful soft feather,
From that day my eyes are hooked on to you,
Feels like a boat dancing in sea blue,
Please show some mercy, don't stop my gaze,
It cuts my soul in many ways,
I will guard you like a kohl guarding your eye,
Let me make your beautiful feathers fly,
You set me on fire when you rub your rosy cheek,
Makes my poor heart go even weak,
Darling! I cant help but fall for you,
How the heaven is surviving without you,
You are like the land shimmering with moon light,
Which takes the beauty to a different height,
You are like a peacock dancing in a garden of flowers,
To whom I can just gaze for hours,
I cant describe your elegance in words,
Look of yours pulls all of my chords,
Yet, you don't react the slightest, girl,
Always glimmer like a graceful pearl,
You are divinity's supreme art,
Every time you touch, it stops my **HEART...**

Stress

It is a **CRAZY** feeling,
Things get tough to be dealing,
Sunshine looks far away through the glass ceiling,
Fearful of an arrow with white feathers,
Creating a broader smile on the ace archers,
Changes the way I look at all weathers,
Forcing myself to build the anxiety,
Doubtful whether I can make a name in the society,
No matter if kindness & patience is my only property,
Egoism, and shallowness of love darken everything,
Smoothness from warmth starts slipping,
Suddenly feels like everything is demolishing,
Pressure grows deeper day by day,
Peace of mind stays far away,
Praying to Almighty for the hope of ray,
I am sure there will be a new light,
Taking away all of this fright,
There will be sunshine to this dark night,
Oh Dear Lord! please shower your bless,
To ring the jingles of success,
Which will take out the **STRESS...**

Struggle

I got a **CRAZY** pleasant laugh,
When I first saw your photograph,
Felt like the beautiful sea was wrapped in pink nectar,
Everyone's desire to be hitched to your wagon star,
She looked like a dais shining like the moon,
She is certainly Almighty's boon,
She is an example of beauty & confidence,
Entire society is enthralled by her amazing existence,
Her presence lights up everything like a Christmas tree,
She gets energy from a small cup of coffee or tea,
She doesn't hesitate to swim against the stream,
Just happiness in all is her only dream,
A girl filled with stars in eyes & a lot of pride,
Always ready to take the throne onto her side,
Loyalty, Love & Support is what she desires,
Which will let her pull the nuptial wire,
An angle who likes humans who write,
She has a persona of bright light,
Why didn't I realize this before,
Certainly better late than never,
Hoping someone to let this time smuggle,
Not meeting this beautiful angel will be anyone's
STRUGGLE...

Flower

I was out in the **CRAZY**town,
When she came like the rain pouring down,
Waiting for her warmth to pour,
But she vanished like water vapor,
When I see, I feel like staring at her,
Her eyes has the power to give dizziness to liquor,
Her mesmerizing scent is in the air,
She is a synonym of care,
Seeing her cheeks, I feel like kissing them,
They look like world's most desirable gem,
Seeing a small thread of hair waving on her forehead,
My heart drops me in to cupid's red,
Seeing her beautiful feet, I dream of becoming her anklets,
Her one look at me puts me in a lot of sweat,
Will entire life be enough to appreciate her beautiful face,
She is a beauty goddess whom everyone wants to embrace,
On a beautiful evening, I strive to walk with her on the streets,
Thinking of the same faster my heart beats,
When I see her, I wish she will have me tied to her by eyes,
To this mother nature she is Divinity's ultimate surprise,
Entire World is hypnotized in her care & love shower,
Her astounding beauty blooms the earth like a
FLOWER...

Music

It is a **CRAZY** weather today,
Our eye contact took my breath away,
This heart has become restless,
Thanking GOD for this beautiful bless,
Currently, there is neither melody nor rhythm,
Life is a messed up algorithm,
Today the rain has drenched me,
Feels like stuck between the devil and deep blue sea,
Oh Lord, my embarrassment has drowned me,
With you I want to create the magical love spree,
It's pouring so much, standing here I think,
Is it time for me to blink???,
I am sure I have lost something, what have I lost,
Trying to keep my fingers crossed,
I admit that we are unknown to each other,
But we will get to know each other,
The condition you are in, that's the condition I am in,
It feels like mesmerizing sound of violin,
Someone tells me from within,
Our voyage together will be classic,
When the world will listen to our love **MUSIC...**

Commitment

It was a **CRAZY**beautiful thing we had,
We were completely in to each other and truly mad,
Oh life, there were some distances between you and me,
but why?
You were the apple of my eye,
How will I now make the feathers fly,
Oh life, the troubles we had,
But the solution to it made both of us glad,
Which you and me have solved together,
Which made me a bird of different feather,
I followed your gestures and kept walking,
Ignoring everyone I kept talking,
I kept walking following your signals,
Kept writing our eventful journals,
Creator of existence had different plans,
Gave me breath but took my life to join hands,
We have met over hundreds of times before,
I swear I can't snore anymore,
Still why do you see me like a stranger?
Your lovely companion is my only hunger,
Let us choose and build a new home,
It's time for me to sleep next to your tomb,
Thank you Almighty for being the arranger,
Finally our paths are colliding into one another,
I promise I will do all the adjustment,

Meeting my life is a different sort of excitement,
Ultimately I am coming out of the banishment,
Loving & being with you through out life and beyond is
my only **COMMITMENT...**

Feel

How many **CRAZY** things come to remembrance,
Those were filled with pure elegance,
How do I forget them,
Eagerly waiting to be with the beautiful gem,
What do I tell my heart?
Waiting to get a flying start,
There are so many things to be said,
Which are stuck on the lips as if afraid,
Why was the story not completed?
Why is it not concreated yet?
How deserted is this atmosphere,
An unknown sorrow revolves there,
On meeting you today, the heart remembered things of
yesterday,
Sight of yours in green took my breath away,
When you looked at me a hope has risen,
Want to get that sense again & again,
You are a beauty of desire,
Who can pull every single wire,
My caravan of heart turns and looks back,
Touch of yours puts it out of track,
Your mesmerizing beauty could put anyone on to kneel,
You are not just an angel, you are a **FEEL...**

Marriage

It was a **CRAZY** time,
When I saw you for the first time,
She looked like a moon without flaw,
Which put my heart in to a beautiful sea-saw,
Things are not the same after that day,
Waiting for the loneliness to fade away,
All flowers are jealous when they look at her,
Because everyone's gaze is drawn to her,
I asked the Almighty how can you make someone so perfect,
GOD replied, sending her to earth is the only thing I regret,
Time filled in the warmth between us,
A lot blessings is what we want for us,
Now is the season of separation,
We will definitely reach our love destination,
It's a guest for a couple of moments,
Soon we will make our union announcements,
From there on it will be only love,
For that I always Thank the Divinity beyond & above,
You are my Honor, Respect & Pride,
Presence of yours gives me strength to go over any tide,
I am sure we will be each other's emotion carriage,
When You & Me become WE in our **MARRIAGE...**

Promise

It was a **CRAZY** weather,
When you knocked me down with a feather,
You arrived like an angel of my dream,
You put my life into an amazing colorful scheme,
This world is a little pale compared to you,
You are the Ambassador of the beautiful sky blue,
What is a fragrance useful for,
Which doesn't match up with the scent of your,
What a color is useful for,
When it doesn't match beautiful lips of your,
Don't hide your beautiful eyes with your eyelid,
Let our future be love amid,
Sign your name on my hands,
With your beautiful hands,
I will circle every moment in your orbit,
The way earth circles in Sun's orbit,
Even if you shatter me into pieces & bits,
Still I will not be calling it quits,
You are mine as long as my name is there in the world,
Will always try to keep you pearled,
There won't be any question of compromise,
I will always be with you, that's my **PROMISE...**

Home

It is a **CRAZY**place,
Where we are always in grace,
A place where we have grown our wings,
There will be no detachment to it's strings,
Let's stomp & jump without worrying,
Coz we are in our own comfort ring,
Time & Day are no bar here,
Yet it teaches us to be sincere,
In the far away city of Millennium,
It makes us feel super premium,
At the shore of a sea filled with nectar,
It stands strong being our protector,
It is the epitome of joy,
Where we hold our first toy,
Always stands with us irrespective of the situation,
Teaches us a new meaning of dedication,
It's our own world within the mother earth,
Where our generations take birth,
It always keeps us warm in her room,
Like a mother in her womb,
Even GOD resides here after the holy roam,
A palace we call **HOME...**

Ordinary Boy

It was a beautiful **CRAZY** night,
And eyes were shining in dreams of height,
Gets down from the train in the bright light,
Wishing half of the world to sleep well & don't let the
bedbugs bite,
Enters the arena to make a name in society,
With eyes full of dreams & heart full of anxiety,
A small town juvenile in the city of education,
Does not know the fast line of communication,
Turning into a laughing stock he thrives for liberation,
Stretch of his imagination soon puts him into isolation,
Years pass by, he has lost his confidence to speak,
Spirit is willing but his eagerness is weak,
Tries hard to utilize many techniques,
Determined & focused, tries to come back to winning
streak,
Appointed in a place he starts his professional affair,
Always trying to prove a point puts him into a lot of scare,
Decades pass by, he continues to work,
It's time for him to open the champagne cork,
Together they start putting color to life,
Soon to be faded, it cut through the knife,
All colors became pale & dark,
No one is there with him to take a walk,
Re-gained confidence shattered again,

But scarred this time, realized to beard the lion in his own den,
He stands up holding is head high,
Believes he can make his wings fly,
Prays to GOD for everyone to stay in happiness & joy,
That's the story of an **ORDINARY BOY...**

9 789354 582202